TABLE OF CONTENTS

PART ONE WAYSIDE STORIES

PART TWO POEM BY WAYSIDE

ISBN-13:978-0615438313

ISBN-10:0615438318

Printed in the United States of America

Made in the USA

The information and images in this book are not, to my personal knowledge, easily accessible elsewhere.

See my websites for more information:

http://www.waysidestories.com

http://www.poetrybywayside.com

DEDICATION

This book is dedicated to my family who had great patience and assisted me while putting these Wayside Stories into book form and helped to save and preserve the works.

This book is also dedicated to the original writer, William McFarland, 'Wayside' who lived in the United States of America in various states from 1823 to 1887.

FORWARD

All references to places, cities, businesses, names, people both past, present and future, are all fictional or imaginary and are not real and simply coincidental.

The information is provided on an as-is basis and is for entertainment purposes only. The author and publisher shall have neither the liability nor responsibility to any person(s) or entity with respect to any loss or damages arising from the stories, works, poems, or any information contained in this book.

May "The Glory World And Guiteau" book be entertaining and a delight to all and bring happiness to the soul. The cover images are from the actual original book from the 1800s. The works are FICTION and like an imaginary world. It's a fictional story written about politics in the late 1800s and about the original writer's feelings when President Garfield was shot and killed by the late Charles Guiteau and the trial of Charles Guiteau afterwards. Remember the original writer was still living at the time of the event and it must have been very hard on him as well as everyone else in the world at the time. This would have been written at a time shortly after the event and this might shed some light into truths not known before. It is very thought provoking and interesting writings in my opinion. There are some topics here about religion and Heaven and Hell, immortality and the hereafter in "The Glory World And Guiteau."

There is political intrigue and a mystery of history of olden times of President Garfield and Charles Guiteau for history buffs as well as religious inspiration. This book was written in the late 1800's and I have typed it like it was handwritten then to the best of my ability from the original manuscript which is now an antique it being over 100 years old and not published in a book form to the best of my knowledge.

Part 2 consists of three more thought-provoking stories. One is Pisgah Or The Great Resolvent and talks of Salvation and the next story is called Machine Prayer which is also political in nature from the 1800s and talks about The Machine and mentions President Garfield, Arthur and Guiteau. The last story in this book is The Machine and The Golden Calf, which is also about The Machine and politics. These probably were all written around the time of the death of Garfield and the trial of Guiteau. If you are a lover of history and/or politics, you should like these stories.

These WAYSIDE STORIES mentioned above were also written in the late 1800s using a quill pen and were also written by a real person William McFarland, one of my ancestors, whose pen name was 'Wayside.' Some of this is so very thought provoking and some of it could have been written yesterday! It may shed some light into the way things were in the late 1800s.

The last two stories were also taken from the same original, handwritten manuscript that "The Glory World And Guiteau" came from. These last few Wayside Stories contained in this book were also kept hidden and preserved for over 100 years in my family. May they never be hidden again. May they be shared and treasured by all. May my family share the Wayside Stories and poems with their own family members. This way they can see some of their great, great, great grandpa's original handwritings by viewing the images contained in this book and they may all have their own personal copy of at least part of their family's heirloom. After this long William McFarland has a lot of descendents many of which I have no idea who or where they are. I hope some of them will also find their ancestor's collection of stories and poems by reading this book as well as other good books by William McFarland 'Wayside.'

The poem, "The Machine", at the end was also written long ago in the late 1800s. This poem was written as well by my great, great, great grandpa, William McFarland 'Wayside.' It talks about politics at the time and has similar themes to "The Glory World and Guiteau." It is added to this book as it is on the same topic as the rest and this way the reader can read one of the poems which William McFarland 'Wayside' had originally written. I simply transcribed them to the best of my ability and typed them as well as adding the images.

Any photos or images in this book are the actual photos that I have taken recently of the ORIGINAL handwriting by a quill pen and the cover of the actual manuscript the words were written in a simple notebook over 100 years ago and thus are a part of my family legacy and are a part of my family's heirloom from many generations.

This actual original book is now yellowed and falling apart so it must be preserved in printed form. This writer was very intelligent and had gorgeous handwriting. Both the book cover and the handwriting in the photos are from the late 1800's and are thus a part of HISTORY and history buffs should enjoy this book especially anyone that likes the story of Garfield and Guiteau and/or politics in the late 1800s, as well as anyone that is into political humor or satire.

This book is part of a collection of short fictional stories and poems written by Wayside and thus I am calling them "Wayside Stories."

Please see my websites:

http://www.waysidestories.com

http://www.poetrybywayside.com

http://www.gloryworldandguiteau.com

http://www.silenceinheavenandthebutterwoman.com

OTHER GOOD BOOKS

BY

WILLIAM McFARLAND

'WAYSIDE'

There is also another book full of fictional *Wayside* Stories entitled, "Silence In Heaven And The Butter-Woman And Other *Wayside* Stories" which was also originally written in the late 1800s by William McFarland "Wayside and came from the same family heirloom." This book has many creative stories in it on various topics as well as some of William McFarland's poetry. This book is also jam packed full of images from the actual original writings. This book was kept with the other poems and stories and William McFarland also wanted those stories and poems printed into a book as well.

There are also another books entitled, "Poetry By Wayside" which features many more poems which William McFarland 'Wayside' had originally written in the late 1800s. This book also has many images from the actual original writings. There actually are three books going along the theme of Poetry By Wayside Book One, Poetry By Wayside Book Two, and Poetry By Wayside Book Three. These poems William McFarland also wanted printed into a book and so this is just what I am doing.

May the writings of William McFarland, a/k/a Wayside, who was also a school teacher besides being a writer, also be an inspiration to family genealogists everywhere to find out more about their ancestors and learn of their lives and history. May my ancestor, William McFarland, be proud!! This has been a labor of love!! It has been my longing for years to have his works published and printed into a book. It is finally happening thanks to self publishing. William McFarland originally wished his works to be published into a book but he died before he could accomplish this task.

May "The Glory World And Guiteau by Wayside" go down in history as it was originally intended many years ago by the original writer, William McFarland.

May you enjoy the photos of the actual stories some of which were copied into this book using my digital camera. Look below for a photograph of the old cover of the handwritten manuscript which was actually used by Wayside and preserved for years by my family.

The information is provided on an as-is basis for entertainment purposes only. The authors, current owners, copyright holder and publishers shall have neither the liability nor responsibility to any person or entity with respect to any loss or damages arising from the stories, poem, images, or any information contained in this book.

INTRODUCTION

This imaginary, fiction original works in this book were kept hidden and preserved for several generations of my family now deceased, and is now being offered for the general public to read and enjoy in printed book form.   Remember the handwritten old script writings here were written in the late 1800's and thus it is over 100 years old. They are unique. I do not think you would find these stories anywhere else. This is a rarity to find such works from long ago which was kept safe for over a hundred years by my family and myself and not printed in book form by the family and very few have seen its actual original handwriting and contents besides family members to my knowledge.

I was the next one chosen to receive the original writings of Wayside in 1993 as I was the one that was doing family history and I was contacting various family members. Upon learning that one of my direct ancestors was a writer I had to find his writings before they were lost. Fortunately for me and my whole family I did locate finally the person that had the stories and poems written by William McFarland 'Wayside' and thus we have kept them hidden and protected until I had time and means to publish them into a book. With the fast speed of the internet and home computers I feel it is a perfect time for me to do this work. There was not time nor opportunity to do this before.

The Glory World And Guiteau
by Wayside

About The Original Author

William McFarland was a writer as well as he was a school teacher. His pen name was Wayside. He was a real person. He lived from 1823 to 1887. This is the year 2011 that I am printing this book. A lot has changed since then. William McFarland was also an officer in the Civil War of the United States of America. William McFarland 'Wayside' has waited a very long time for his book to be published. This book is part it. William McFarland was married and had three daughters, one of whom was my great, great grandmother. He was married to Anna Virginia Donaldson, my great, great, great grandmother on that side of the family. One of their daughters, Elizabeth McFarland Wicks, was my great, great grandmother on that side of the family.

The Glory World And Guiteau
by Wayside

The Glory World

And

Guiteau

The Glory World And Guiteau
by Wayside

PART ONE

CHAPTER ONE

The Glory World

And Guiteau

A Burlesque Satire

By

William McFarland

'Wayside'

Great is the mystery of godliness (Providence) and the grand unknown beyond. How infinitesimally small must the finite appear when compared to the infinite; and how incomprehensibly great must be the mind that is able to grasp the Universe. The Philosophy of a future state has never been fully understood neither has it entered into the heart of man to conceive what is held in reserve for the faithful.

The great study of mankind is the Philosophy of a Future State yet when it is their privilege to see, and hear, and know, for themselves how they tremble and quake with fear because of that which they know not. Their imaginations picture to them a dreadful terror, behind the screen that hides behind the vale beyond. We have tried many times to take a glimpse of The Glory World but always tried in vain because we could not dare to face that dreadful monster. That grisly terror has been held up before the world as a make believe or scare-crow so as to gull the ignorant and hold the feeble-minded stubborn in subjection. For thousands of years this Phantom Terror has been preached so as to hold the world in awe. Also, to give tone and strength to the fundamental principles of Christianity and enlarge and improve our views of God and the Devil; of Hell and Heaven. Also of mankind's future abode in the infernal regions and The Glory World.

The true philosophy of a future state is of Divine inspiration and only found in the Bible; which was written by the finger of God and revealed to us through the Spirit. But oh, how many mistake the Spirit and wander from the truth.

Finite minds were not made to grasp Infinity. Neither can they measure the habiliments of The Glory World with a yard-stick. Nor say to Providence, "Why doest Thou so?" We are only to live, and let live. Take God at His word; pray without ceasing, never weary in well doing but study the Word and watch the developments of light (progress).

Mankind is full of desire which cannot be satisfied with things of time and sense; but like some lost planet revolving through space still keeps wandering. He searches every nook and corner of God's creation for the lost link, or the hidden mystery, that connects this with the world beyond. There is no device on this side of the grave that reveals things eternal. Mankind is very superstitious and exceedingly nervous on this question; when he is approached and called to go, he trembles all over, for if caught looking behind the veil, he knows full well that he will not be permitted to return and his place of abode on the other side is that which troubles him most, for he doesn't know on which side of the rock of Adamant it will be. My desires kept increasing in magnitude, until I longed for something more tangible and real. I prayed that the veil might be lifted, that I might take a glimpse of The Glory World and the future state. My eyes wandered over the world. I saw, and felt the depravity of the human heart. The love of money was the root of all evil, and the desire for wealth and power in the world was so great that mankind would stoop to anything, no matter how wicked it was, so he could gain the coveted prize. I felt surely perplexed. Was mankind made in vain? Did God make a mistake, or was he trying to make a corner on man and get swindled by the Devil? These kind of thoughts were very perplexing, and bothered me continually.

The world is full of trickery and deception and most all have a way of their own. Many were calling to their fellows saying, "This is the way;" but everyone has a road of his own, and no two are alike. These roads were all denominated the grand Highway to Heaven and so straight that no crooked thing could walk therein! It was hard for me to understand about so many "Ways" when I was informed by all of them, that there was only one way, and theirs was the true and only "Straight Way to Heaven."

But I found it a difficult matter to walk in any of these ways because they were so very crooked and besides this there were so many branches that seemed to be going the same way. Nobody could tell which was the right way. The Highway of Holiness is a straight and narrow way, but, I found this one chuck full of bits thieves, robbers and snares and so very crooked you could hardly find one quarter of a mile throughout its whole length where it was perfectly straight or even safe to walk in.

Another thing that worried me much and caused me to doubt the authenticity of the scriptures was this; I found the Highway filled with murderers, thieves, cut throats and robbers, who as a privilege would sometimes be permitted to take a short cut to The Glory World, via the gallows. I rather envied them their quick transit to The Glory World yet at the same time I did not admire the mode of conveyance.

I have sometimes thought there was no such thing as a future state. That this world was all there was of it. I could not understand what good there was in the Lake of Fire and the Second Death; neither could I see how a man could die twice and still live. I thought it was trouble enough to die once without being bothered again. Neither could I see what good sense there was in killing a man twice. What good, what pleasure can there be in raising up an old toper who had died with snakes in his boots just to kill him again?

What a mockery these things all appeared to be. I could neither believe nor understand such things. Infidelity was fast taking hold of me. Things here below were in a terrible muddle. The martyred remains of the dead president lie mouldering at mentor while the assassin was about to pay the penalty on the scaffold. Although he claimed and protested to the last moment that he was innocent that it was God who did it to save the Republican party from ruin and the country from going to perdition.

This was a strange doctrine, so full of the incomprehensible that a poor - ignorant mortal like me could not possibly understand. But Providence knowing my honesty of heart and feeling inclined to be generous concluded to relieve the suspense by giving me a free pass to The Glory World and return ticket. This trip opened my eyes and caused me to see clearly. It was then and there I was furnished the proof of how things was run above and who are the honored and respected ones of The Glory World. I was there taught to believe that all things are possible. That the meanest man on earth can be made the greatest saint in The Glory World. The happiest man above, and the one who shines the brightest will be one of the dirtiest villains of earth, who has been washed and cleansed the most! Just like the Prodigal Son who strayed away from home and spent all his efforts in debauchery and riotous living, was more respected by his father than the son who stayed at home and never was known to do wrong, or even get drunk. This may seem strange doctrine to the people of this world. But to the Christian, he believes it for the very Word's sake. Read your Bibles, search the scriptures, and then you can see and believe. I believe it for the Bible was written by the finger of God and no man can do that for they all have to use a pen.

Great is the mystery of Godliness, and worthy is the man who is able to find the path and then walk in it. But greater is the man that can use it politically for his reward shall be great in the kingdom, for he was a stalwart of the Stalwarts and suffered martyrdom for the good of his party. He shall sit on the right hand of the Father and the Blainites and Half-Breeds shall be his servants.

It is very difficult for mankind to believe the truth all the time. There are so many strange things that happen contrary to our wishes and desires, and expectations and apparently so ridiculous we are compelled to doubt. Even Providence, with all his wisdom, knowledge and power for awhile seems scarcely to know what to do. Some people presume to say that he knew it all the time; that whatever came to hap was fore-ordained and could not be helped! But I think if he had known the serpent was going to defile Mother Eve by robbing the first woman in the universe of her virtue; He would have watched things a little closer by keeping a sharper eye on the Devil.

Our preachers tell us many curious and strange things which are hard to believe. Yet we must believe for the preacher says it is God's word and we all know that God can't lie for the preacher says so. But I must quit this kind of philosophical twaddle and leave the doctrine of free salvation to the Priests. I must hasten with my narrative and give you an account of that wonderful vision of The Glory World, the discoveries there made, and what grand demonstration was made in favor of Saint Guiteau's arrival who had just made the passage from the scaffold to the kingdom. Guiteau who perished on the scaffold as a martyr for his party and for his country's good was persecuted and tormented by the people; even his own party went back on him, and let him die the ignoramus death of an assassin, never interfering in his behalf, not raising a finger in objection. His enemies after they had killed him had him dissected and all his flesh scraped from the bones and burned. Then his anatomy was riveted and wired together, and then sold at public auction to the highest bidder and the proceeds were dedicated to the party and put where they thought it would do the most good. That is the way they served one whom the Lord which I saw in my vision delighted to honor. A full and true report of the grand finale in the courts above was faithfully and correctly chronicled by "Wayside" for he was there and saw it all.

On Friday, June 30, about noon feeling much depressed in body and mind, I wandered forth in search of something I knew not what. In a listless pensive mood, I still wandered on, brooding over things uncertain and the future state feeling weary and tired almost to death I ascended a little knoll, fell prostrate to the earth and tried to pray.

My swift journey up through the Boundless Blue, without labor, without toil or exertion, was thrilling indeed. It seemed to me like the dreams of all my early childhood, when I would sometimes stretch my arms and sail away to unknown lands. As we journeyed on through the Stellar plain we passed Mars, Jupiter, Saturn, Uranus and Neptune, whose rapid movement was snail-like, when compared to ours.

On our way up through the "Eternal Blue" I found a host of others who looked as if they were bending all their energies to get there first. I inquired of one of the principal leaders, "What was it that caused them to make such haste?" He answering said, "We are going to the Celestial city, as special envoys, and to report the proceedings. Saint Guiteau will be there in less than an hour. We want to be there in time to view the Grand Pageant that escorts him up to the gates.

Then, as if greater powers were given, we soared on swifter wings and soared to our own Native Heaven. In a moment of time, much less than the time it takes to describe, we were there standing within the Gates of Pearl. And as the inner gates swung open on their golden hinges, we passed into the Holy of Holies, where all the dignitaries of the Church Triumphant were congregated. Oh! What a sight greeted my vision. The grandeur, glory, and magnificent display of things eternal were beyond the power of mind to contemplate or describe. My astonished vision was lost in wonder, and amazement at the astonishing and magnificent display of things innumerable in The Glory World.

And when the curtains rose what a vast crowd! O! My! Greeted my vision. O my! There were Angels and Archangels. There were Seraphim and Cherubims, with all the martyrs, and all the saints and just men made perfect; a host innumerable. I saw Saint John the Divine there and he told me that this was the same crowd he saw in prophetic vision from the Isle of Patmos. There were thousands of thousands and ten times thousands. A vast multitude, which no man could number.

"But, why are they all standing so near the gates?" said I. He replied, "We are all stationed by the Order of our Superior Commander so as to give elate to the occasion, and a fitting and proper welcome to Saint Guiteau. The Great Republican martyr whose arrival is momentarily expected. We ascended the Grand Observatory and arranged ourselves in order so as to have a better view of the approaching Hero, and the grand escort, which was plainly visible in the distance. Everyone was standing tiptoed around the parapet, watching from the Battlements of Heaven the near approach of the grand ouve leade and its conquering Hero, whose snowy white plume waved gracefully in the distance. The intensity of feeling was supreme every eye diluted, and expanded, wider and wider as the Grand Escort rounded up to the Gates. In an instant Heaven's Artillery were let loose in one grand salute, which reverberated throughout the Vaulted Dome and shaking the universe to its centre. Then the Bells began a merry peal, and the rich, sweet harp-strings of The Glory World were raised to the highest key. The organ's notes of the Grand Cathedral chimed in unison and filled the Vaulted Dome with the richest and sweetest melodies of Heaven. Mine eyes were ravished with delight and strained to their utmost tension on viewing the approaching of the Conquering Hero and his noble escort. All were draped in long white robes and riding white horses as their long white robes fluttered in the breeze, they seemed as Angel's wings enveloping a Heavenly transparency of snowy invisibility.

An advance courier came dashing up in front on his snowy white charger, and said, "Prepare to receive the Lord's Anointed for Saint Guiteau is at hand."

All arose, and with heads uncovered stood awaiting the supreme moment. Closer and closer they came all in complete order keeping step with the music of the spheres.

Just then I saw that which astonished me most - that which I could not understand. A little in advance of the rest came Guiteau and Garfield the two grand opposing forces in the world below now sitting side by side in an open carriage rejoicing together.

Sorrows and troubles in the world below. That the great break in the Republican Party was healed. That all jarring factions in our ranks after this would cease to trouble and the country would be saved. The grand carriage in which to two noted worthies rode up to the Gate was the most splendid that could be thought of and beautifully numbered in large golden letters just the same. No I used to see everywhere marked in the world below. I thought it was a strange coincident. Could it be possible that a Democrat had crawled in to Glory World while the guards slept and numbered the carriage? But I was soon informed by one that knew, that this was a mark of distinction, which none of the truly Loyal were permitted to wear.

This notable carriage was drawn by twelve large white stallions gaily caparisoned kept constantly champing their bits. At the word of command the mighty crowd moved on. While all around, above, below, and on every side, swarmed the guards of Honor, and the innumerable retinue that followed in their wake.

The National Band of The Glory World that only plays on special occasions was detailed as a special favor, and played the grand march, "Hail to the Chief," in honor of Saint Guiteau's safe and glorious arrival.

I could not help but think, how strange; how passing strange that Providence would stoop so low as to notice of such a worthless creature as Guiteau was reported to be. I had supposed from what I had heard said at his trial in the world below, that he was totally depraved and unworthy of the least particle of respect whatever. The Half-Breeds, Feather-heads and ministers of the gospel said he was of his father the devil; that he could have neither part nor lot in The Glory World. I remembered that the Church would not even pray for him. Nor would they visit him when sick or in prison except an old carpet bagger (Preacher) who was also reported to be as mean and wicked as Guiteau; who had killed The Lord's anointed, President Garfield, the best man in the world that he was a disgrace to the Republican party and the age in which he lived that he should cast anchor from the rope's end to the hottest corner in Hell and be damned eternally. These kind of words or expression were bourn on every breeze and by every Half-Breed and Chronic Saint in the land. Except it were those wicked Stalwarts that had got left behind at the convention, and the blood-thirsty Democrats. They conspired together and all tried to save his life by saying he was crazy. Garfield incurred the displeasure of the Democrats, because he was one of those visiting Christian Statesmen who so cleverly took them in and swindled them out of the Presidency by politely playing false, and getting that old ignorant Negro woman Eliza Pinkston to swear falsely for the sake of the Republican party and their immediate salvation and to the rejection of the wicked Democrats. The Stalwarts said Garfield did not deserve their favor neither, for he had been false to them after election by not giving them the offices. They deserved all the offices, for it had not been for their aid and almost superhuman exertion the Republican Party would have sank out of sight. For Garfield without the Stalwarts was nowhere. The large Stalwart Purse of Brady's and Dorsey's done the work and done it well. Everybody knows that Dorsey was the Savior of Indiana. It was Dorsey's scientific strategy and maneuvering that made the grand turning point that gave us the victory. The Half-Breeds and Feather-heads may talk and say what they please but if it had not been for the Stalwarts and the Dorseys where would the Republican Party be today. This is why the Lord remembers

Guiteau and has exalted his horn among all the Saints in The Glory World. But I must return to that part of the subject that relates to the final entrance and reception given within the gates. The grand medley of spiritual combination was far above my comprehension. I could not understand things Divine. Nor could I reconcile them in my own mind. There was such a sacred medley in the religion and politics of The Glory World that soared above my comprehension. I thought many things. Did Providence make a mistake, or is it possible for him to blunder? Did he misapprehend, or had he been misinformed? Had he not been imposed by some shewed Stalwart spirit who had gotten up this great demonstration in favor of Guiteau just to beat the Half-Breeds by bribing. Providence like they did the Half-Breeds in the world below and then impose on his good nature. But soon the scales fell from my eyes and I saw clearly.

Things in The Glory World are somewhat like they are here. Providence like the preachers always adopts the popular side. It does not matter who wins, he is always found on top.

But I must hasten with my narrative which still increases in interest the most sublime as they roll in lofty grandeur through the gates. Every avenue of approach was crowded to the utmost. The vast multitude swaying back and forth still increasing in intensity. Each one striving to be near enough so as to touch the hem of his garment, because they all believed there was virtue in him. The great high walls of the eternal city were densely packed with spiritual beings waiting the supreme moment when the gates should open.

As the watchman and guards on the wall presented arms to the advancing Hero the Heavenly doors gave way and the beautiful Gates of Pearl revolved on their golden hinges, when all marched into the City together.

Grandly waved the flag of the Universe as we rounded Capitol Hill while the chorus of ten thousand voices was taken up by the hills in fresh echoes of the song of welcome. A monster meeting was held in the public park of the great city. On an elevated plateau in the middle of the park were three Golden Cushions on which were seated viz. Providence in the middle, Guiteau on the right and Garfield on the left while the high dignitaries of Church and State filled the background. Being somewhat of a privileged character I was permitted to sit on an elevated plateau. On looking around carefully and scanning everything closely so as to gather all the news of importance. I discovered a small cluster of Half Breeds in the farthest corner consulting together in whispers. They were very much excited and all appeared in deep trouble because they knew not what to say or do. They did not like the turn of affairs this change of front. This glorious reception and grand display made for the special benefit of Guiteau and the Stalwart Spirits, was not what they wanted, for Guiteau was a poor miserable sinner, and for the atrocious and most outrageous murder of Garfield deserved the lowest and hottest corner in Hell. But to be honored beyond his deserts, and extolled above his peers was truly mortifying. And his final reception by the highest Dignitaries of the Church Triumphant in the Courts of Heaven took them all by surprise. It certainly was more than they had bargained for. So they sank into the shadow of the wall and wrote to Blaine; asking him how they should conduct themselves, and what they should do about it. His answer came promptly, and to the point. It came by spiritual telegraph and read thus, "When you live in Providence you must do as Rome does, and if Heaven booms for Guiteau, you must boom for him too." This was certainly hard on the Half-Breeds, but there was no other way out of the dilemma. So they all fell down and worshipped at the Shrine of Guiteau, saying "Great is Guiteau and great is Arthur whom he made President. The Lord is our God for he rewardeth the Stalwarts. Guiteau was a Saint, one worthy to be remembered and honored for his good services to the Republican Party." Then they all shouted aloud, "Glory to God, Guiteau, and the Machine for great is the mystery of godliness, the Church, and the machine, for their ways are past finding out."

As I sat close by on an elevation watching the change of scene who should make his appearance at this instant but the Great War Governor of Indiana. He was carried in on a Divan of the finest silk. Providence arose and made him acquainted with Saint Guiteau the honored martyr of the Great Republican Party. The great war governor arose and pressed Guiteau to his bosom and said, "Blessed is the light of thy countenance and thy reward is great. The Lord delighteth to honor such and thy rewards shall be still greater than these. When the great war governor made this remark his face shown like the seven different colors of the Rainbow and his voice fell on the assembled multitude like the mighty rumbling of the waters. There was a sublimity and grandeur in it.

The War Governor was a splendid looking saint whose physique was excellent, all but the legs. They were very spindling and weak, caused him to weary while standing long.

Those spindle legs of his were caused by an indiscretion in his youthful days. A strange woman in the great and wicked city of Baltimore had lain hold of him and dragged him to her house where she beguiled him. I presume she was one of those Midianitish women that caused Israel to sin; you know they were real handsome and so very enticing that he couldn't withstand the pressure of their voluptuous charm. The Lord looked in mercy on him, forgave him freely and made him an apostle and sat him on high among the saints, but his legs would never grow to their proper size so the smaller saints had to carry him about on his Palace Divan. These things were given him on account of his war record, while Governor of Indiana. But the most remarkable event of the War Governor was after his ascension when he was received into the Holy of Holies. Providence seeing he was a cripple and being full of compassion at that moment, turned to his son, Jesus Christ. Said Arise, and let the Great War Governor of Indiana have your seat, for he is one of the noble few who died in the faith in the world below. "Let us give the War Governor such a reception that will astonish Glory World.

The scenes enacted there in the park passed in quick review before me. Time will not permit me to give a full detail, neither would it be possible to even name the many notables, high dignitaries that made their presence known. A few more will suffice for the present.

The most beautiful and sublime attraction, one that vied with stars of the first magnitude was witnessed when the veteran Saint Zach Chandler in company with a noted Seraphim, Eliza Pinckston, made their appearance. There was joy in the heart, light in the eyes, and music in the soul, for it was Eliza's false oath four years before and the strong protestations of Old Zach that saved the Republican Party from utter destruction.

These two notable worthies were given the privileges of the Kingdom and were permitted to roam over the city at will and feast on whatever they saw or the soul desired. They were both patron Saints and because they were both dear lovers of the stimulant in the world below, privilege was given them to carry a small flask of the wholesome beverage with them so they could have things handy and take a little for the stomach sake, or whenever they felt like it.

These two notable Saints were very loving and tender towards one another and marched arm in arm around and around the grand pavilion. They both acted as if they were independent in all things and neutral in nothing. But their greatest attraction, that which inspired them the most was the frequent application of the Brandy Bottle to their lips. That gave the greatest amount of inspiration for it made Zach's nose to shine and Saint Eliza so happy she could hardly stand alone. Sometimes they would be so full of the sublime both would have to lie down and rest awhile until the bottle of inspiration was all gone (consumed). But to return to the story while I left off in the park, where the great magistrates of Glory World were congregated. There above the heads of Guiteau and Garfield was plainly written in blazing letters of gold, "These are they who have come up through much tribulation and have made their robes white by much washing. Their record in the world below is a bright one, one worthy of the highest distinction. Now what shall be done to him whom the Lord delighted to honor? Soon a resolution was put and carried by acclamation; that the one whom the Lord delighteth to honor the most should be elevated and made conspicuous that he should be paraded through the streets on horseback on one of the Lord's finest stallions. Draped up in one of the Lord's best Sunday suits with a golden crown on his head, the whole outfit to be of the very best and extremely gorgeous. Also one of the Lord's most notable servants should be appointed to lead the horse through the streets of the city who shall program at the top of his voice to all the people, "Thus shall it be done to him whom the Lord delighteth to honor."

On looking over the vast assembly they discovered the bold and daring spirit of Pine Tree State whose snowy-white Plumes glittered in the distance. He was chosen immediately, and donning his best robes proceeded to perform the required duty by first reporting at headquarters. Providence held out the Golden Scepter and smiled on the advancing Hero for he was the most noble Roman of them all, and said to him, "My son James repine not at Providence, but go and do as required, for we must do nothing more to widen the breach in the Republican Party, for if we antagonize the machine, there will be war in The Glory World, and my throne would be in danger. My dear son James do be careful recollect that the eyes of all are upon you, curb your dislike to such menial service for the Stalwarts have the advantage. If all goes well, and we prove successful in the next genial engagement with the enemies of Glory World, your reward may come sooner than expected. Give ear to the suggestions bow in subjection to the necessities of the situation and trust the rest to Providence. But I would admonish you to pray three times a day with your face turned towards The White House for there is great efficacy in prayer, who knows but what lightning might strike and your horn be exalted among the people. James after listening in deep reverence to the Divine suggestions fell down upon his knees and kissed the greal loe of his Superior Commander. Then he arose and escorted Guiteau all over the city, proclaiming as he went, "This is the way the Lord rewards his servants, and thus shall it be done to him whom the Lord delighteth to honor." But this proud, bold spirit was ill at ease; his very countenance betrayed the inward commotion of his mighty mind. The Goddess of Liberty who was standing close by whispered in his ear as he was passing and said, "Blaine where are you? Have you surrendered too? Recollect "Let no guilty man is watching you, the one that talks horse and is branded on the forehead "Third Term." He scowled upon you as you were passing by and said sneeringly, "What a Gobbler for a Groom." Just then a tall, thin spare looking ghost pops up with grin spread all over his face, looking as wicked as the Devil said, "Dammit, didn't I tell you so?" You hung the wrong man, didn't you? You ought to have known better." This last expression coming from a Stalwart of the Stalwarts was very grinding and bore heavily on the head and heart of the Plumed Knight of the Kennebee. He secretly swore in his heart that he would have satisfaction, that his revenge would be swift and terrible. Just then he saw Guiteau, Garfield and Providence approaching, he put on a sickly smile and presented arms to them while passing and immediately after fell fainting in a fit. A knot of Half Breeds soon gathered around, picked him up and carried him away to his castle, and hid him away in a chamber, there they sprinkled him with holy water and rubbed him well with oil.

But what astonished me most was the indifference of the three great worthies towards the stricken chieftain. They drove right along not even caring to look back when he fell. This kind of treatment to so celebrated a chieftain filled me with sadness. Again I became weary and wandered in the spirit while vision fled before me. I felt like my travels in Glory World were about drawing to a close. The great desire of my heart had been filled. I had seen that which no other living person had been permitted to see. The grand display of the spiritual was so overwhelming I could not hold anymore. The Lord having given me scriptural measure "Pressed down, shaken together, heaping full, and running over" with incomprehensibility of the inexpressible.

It is written in the Old Family Bible that lay on the stand that desire shall fail, not so with me; for mine were increased. I longed to return to the world below, enter that sleeping little body of mine which I left reclining listlessly there on the little knoll, and then report to the press the things I had both seen and heard in The Glory World. I felt it my bounden duty to let the world know that Providence, Guiteau and the Machine were one, and that the Republican Party was the Right Bower of the Machine. Just as this moment while I was absorbed in a deep brown study, pondering over the events just past: A ministering spirit tapped me gently on the shoulder and said, "Wayside, your time is up, and you must away, return and report to the friends below what things you have both seen and heard and let the readers of the tribune be apprised of the facts. Then taking me by the hand he lead me away in the spirit down through the illimitable plaines of the upper deep on the swiftest wings of thought. When I awoke to consciousness I was sitting at my own writing desk just finishing the Narrative of the Wonderful Vision of Glory World And Guiteau and my safe return to earth.

The Glory World & a Guita[r]

[...]is was a strange doctrine; so f[...]
[...] poor ignorant mortal like me c[...]
[...] But providence knowing m[...]
[...] inclined to be genereous "Cone[...]
[...] by giving me a free pass to the c[...]
[...]ip opened my eyes and cauze[...]
[...]nd there I was furnished the f[...]
[...]bove and who are the hono[...]
[...]lory world, I was there too[...]
[...] urepossible. That the one o[...]
[...]de the greatest saint in the[...]

MANY PHOTOS (images) were taken of the story The Glory World And Guiteau which were taken from the original, handwritten documents which were written in the late 1800s by William McFarland (Wayside). I have made these into black and white images for this book. The photos that you see here in this book came from the actual antique writings right from the originals!

...over the world, I saw, and f
the human heart. The love of money
evil, and ~~that~~ the desire for wealth
world was so great that mankin...
any-thing, no matter how wick...
gain the coveted prize. I felt ...
Mankind made in vain? D...
Or was he trying to make a corner
...lled by the Devil? ...kind of...
...lexing, and bothered me Continue...
The world is full of trickery and...

...lled by the Devil? ...kind of...
...lexing, and bothered me Continue...
The world is full of trickery and
all have a way of their own. ...
their fellows saying "This is the...
a road of his own, and no tw...
were all denominated the...
...eaven and go straight the...
...uld walk therein? It wa...
...d about so many" No...

The Glory World & Quite

But I found it a difficult matter to...
ways because they were so very crook...
there were so many branches that seem...
same way. Nobody could tell which...
The Highway of holiness is a straigh...
but I found this one chuck full of...
so very crooked you could har...

...died with snakes in his boots just to...
...of these things all appeared to be, I couldn't...
stand such things. Infidelity was fast...
...Things here below were in a terrible...
...typed remains of the dead president lie...
...erector while the assassin was about...
...on the scaffold. Although he claimed...
the last moment that he was innocent - that...
...ded it to save the Republican party...
...from going to perdition.

the happiest man above, and the one
will be one of the dirtiest villains
and cleanest of the most. Just like
strayed away from home and
debaucheries and riotous living,
his father than the son who stayed
was known to do wrong, or even
This may seem strange Doctrine to the
to the Christian, he believes it for the
Bible, search the scriptures, and then

...saint in the glory
above, and the one who shines the brightest
dirtiest villains of Earth who has been washed
most. Just like the Prodigal Son who
home and spent all his effects in
riotous living, was more respected by
son who stayed at home, and never
wrong, or even get drunk.
Doctrine to the people of this world.
believes it for the very Words sake. Read
scriptures, and then you can see and believe.

...octrine to the people of this nation...
...es it for the very Wordisishe Ready...
...res, and then you can see and believe.
...ble was written by the finger of God...
...for they all have to use apon.
...of godliness, and worthy is the man...
...path and then walk in it. But great...
...e it politically for his reward shall be...
..., for he was a stalwart of the Stalwart...
...isdom for the good of his party. He shall...
...d of the Father and the Plainite... and

Great is the mystery of godliness, and worthy...
...who is able to find the path and then walk in it...
...is the man that can use it politically for his rewa...
great in the kingdom, for he was a stalwart of...
And suffered martyrdom for the good of his pa...
sit on the right hand of the Father and the Bla...
Half-Breeds shall be his servants   the trut...
It is very difficult for mankind to believe all th...
are so many strange things that happen cons...
wishes and desires, and expectations and...
so ridiculous we are compelled to doubt. Even...
with all his wisdom, knowledge and power a...
seems scarcely to know what to do. Some peo...
...they knew it all the time; that what...

was written by the finger of you
they all have to use a pen.
liness, and worthy is the man
it and then walk in it. But great
politically for his reward shall
for he was a stalwart of the Stalwa
n for the good of his party. He sha
to Father and the Blainites an
his servants   the truth

On our way up through the ... Blue ... for
of others who looked as if they were bending all
ges to get there first. I inquired of one of the
pall bearers. What was it that caused them
such hast, he answering said. We
the Celestial city, as Special Envoys, and
the proceedings. Saint Guiteau will ...
than another. We want to be there in tim
the Grand Pageant that escorts him up to
then as if greater power were given, we soared
And soared to our own Native Place. No man
less than the time it takes to describe it, we were there

... as if greater powers were given, we soared or
descended to our own native Heaven. In a moment
... than ... it ... to describe, nor were there
within ... of ... And as the inner gate
on their golden hinges are passed into the ...
all the dignitaries of the church Triumphant were
... Oh, what a sight greet my vision, The
and magnificent display of things Eternal were
... to contemplate or describe. ... aston
lost in wonder, and amazement at the astonish
...ificent display of things innumerable in the ...
And when the curtain rose what a vast ...
greeted my vision, O my! there were Angels, and ...

the grand pavillion. They both acted as ...
pendent in all things and neutral in no...
... attraction, that which inspired them the m...
application of the Brandy Bottle to their
greatest amount of inspiration for it ...
and Saint Eliza so happy she coul...
sometimes they would be so full of th...
have to lie down and rest awhile ...
was all gone." (or some t.)
But to return to the story, where I left ...
... Magnates of Glory World ...

killed him had him dissected
...om the bones and burned
...ted and wired together
...tion to the highest bidder and the
...d to the party and put whe...
...men good, that is the
...m the Lord which Brau...
...honor. A full and true re...
...urts ...ave was faithful

...is father than the son when
was known to do wrong, or
This may seem strange Doctrine
to the Christian, he believes it for
Bible, search the scriptures, and
I Believe it for the Bible was
...no man can do that for they
Great is the mystery of God...

and suffered martyrdom for the g...
sit on the right hand of the Father a...
Half Breeds shall be his servan...
It is very difficult for mankind to...
are so many strange things that...
wishes and desires, and expe...
ridiculous we are compelled to...
with all his wisdom, knowledge...
seems scarcely to know wha...
to say that he knew it all the te...

...le of the scribe. My astonished vision wa...
amazement at the astonishing and mag...
things innumerable in the glory world...
...tains rose what a vast crowd. At next...
...ere were Angels, and Arch angels. There were...
...tims, with all the Martyrs, and all the...
...made perfect, a host innumerable.
the Divine there and ... told me that ...
...saw in prophetic vision from the ...
...thousands of thousands and ten tim...
...multitude which no man could...

These two notable worthies were give[n]
dem and were permitted to roam over
feast on whatever they saw or the soul d[?]
patron saints and because they we[re]
stimulant in the world below, privileg[e]
a small flask of the wholesome beverag[e]
have things handy and take a little
whenever they felt like it
These two notable saints were ve[ry]

and command[ing] them with S. O. for a time a[?]
with a darkness that surrounded its mother ch[?]
only a moment then all was light. Suddenly
opened and the situation was changed. A c[?]
[t]wailed, I cast my eyes eastward and saw the[?]
still like loves wild dream of fond imaginat[ion]
in the distance an angelic being envelop[ed]
whiteness descending from heaven and [?]
passage direct to the spot on the little koll [?]
able to look upon the lustre of his counte[nance]
like the sun I shut my eyes and fe[lt]
heavenly messenger soon came, and t[?]
me to stand up, which I did. [?]
saying, "Wayside, your prayer have[?]

...are the...

I was there taught to believe that all ...that the meanest man on earth can ...saint in the Glory world...

...e, and the one who shines the brightest ...est Villains of Earth who has been washed... ...st. Just like the Prodigal Son who ...home and spent all his effects in ...is living, was more respected by ...n who stayed at home, and never ...ing, or even get drunk.

...oring in his half, not raising a finger in ...nemies after they had killed him had him ...all his flesh scraped from the bones and ...his anatomy was riveted and wired ...en sold at public auction to the highe... ...eeds were dedicated to the party a... ...ought it would do the most good, a... ...they served one whom the Lord... ...esion delighted to honor. As...ll... ...the grand finale in the courts above... ...rrectly chronicled by "Wayside," for he...

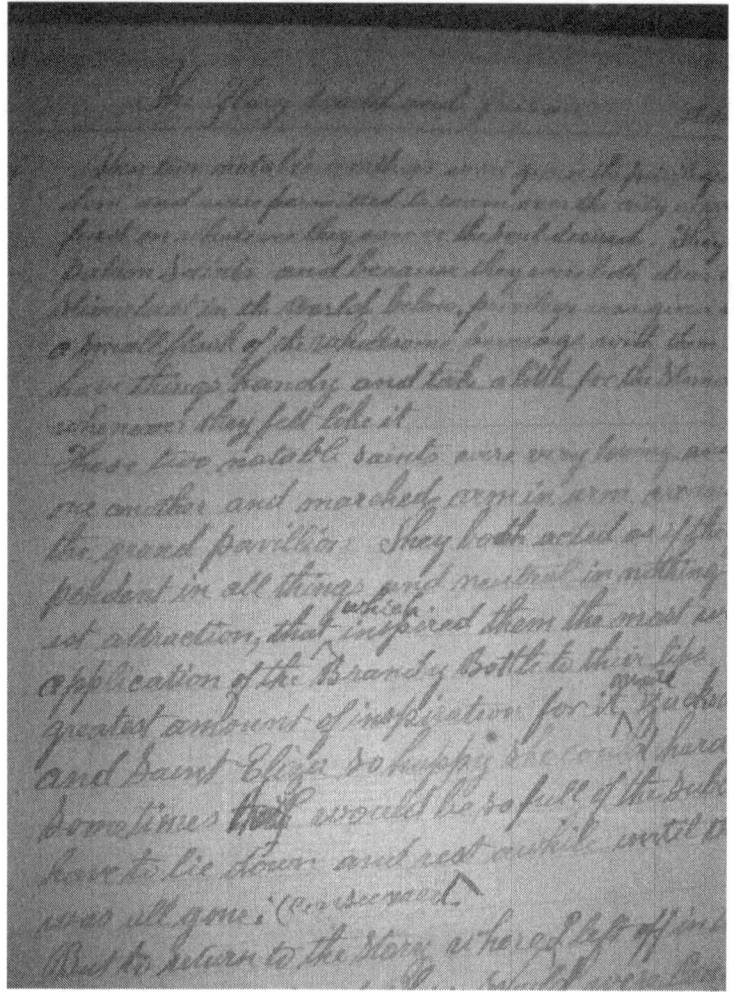

Lovers of Half-Breed and Chronic Saints in the Lord. The wicked Stalwarts that had got left behind at the Convention blood thirsty Democrats. They conspired together and his life by saying he was crazy.

Garfield incurred the displeasure of the Democrats because one of these Visiting Christian Statesmen who so them in and swindled them out of the Presidency by false, and getting that old ignorant Equadorian to swear falsely for the sake of the Republican party salvation and to the rejection of the wicked.

The Stalwarts said Garfield did not deserve their for he had been false to them after election by not offices. They deserved all the offices, for if it had aid and almost superhuman exertion the Republican would have sunk out of sight. For Garfield with was nowhere. The large Stalwarts and Bondage done the work and done it well. Everybody Dorsey was the savior of Indiana. His skillful strategy and maneuvering the ground turning point that gave us the victory heads and feathers heads may talk and but if it had not been for the

... to the mind that is able to grasp ... The Philosophy of a future State has never been fully ... neither has it entered into the heart of man to con... is held in reserve for the faithful.

The great study of mankind is the Philosophy of ... Yet when it is their ... to see, and hear, and know, ... how they tremble and quake with fear because ... they know not. Their imaginations picture to the "Terror,", behind the screen that hides the vale bey... tried many times to take a Glimpse of the Glory ... ways tried in vain because ... could not ... dreadful monster; that grisly Terror has been ... world as a make believe or Scare-Crow so as ... ignorant and hold the feeble-minded in subjection, ... years this ... Terror has been ... to hold the world in subjection. Also, to ... and strength to the fundamental princip... tianity and enlarge and improve ... God and the Devil, of Hell and of ... of mankinds future abode in the ... gion, and the "Glory World."

The true philosophy of a future State is ... ... and only found in the Bible; ...
... the ... of God and ...

CHAPTER TWO

WAYSIDE STORIES

PISGAH OR THE GREAT RESOLVENT

BY

WILLIAM McFARLAND

'WAYSIDE'

Mount Pisgah is a sublime place, and very high. It is from here the favored few are permitted to see the Land of Promise. Many are its votaries who try to climb the height sublime. But long before they reach the dizzy height, their faith fails them. But a large slough of muddy water which surrounds the base has a wonderful affect on the optic nerve if applied outwardly, which enables them to see the Land of Promise from most any place. The name of this slough resolvent is called salvation. It is shallow and muddy and its smell is very offensive, but nevertheless it is a great watering place. The curative powers of this slough water is truly wonderful; no matter how filthy you are, it will make your garments appear whiter than snow. Those who use that water need never use soap. I have known many who would steal and lie for Christ sake, do all manner of deviltry and wallow in all kinds of filth and corruption; and with one dose of this slough salvation resolvent applied externally would be made to shine as bright as the moon day sun. The workings of trickery and jugglery which has been carried on for years has brought many a soul to poverty and rags by the professed followers of Christ. I doubt scarcely understand it. But after taking in the great slough which flows from the side of the hill and seeing its wonderful effects I knocked under; I surrendered; I admitted that salvation was the grand exponent of reform. It could make black; white, and white black. If there was anything too filthy to be seen or known by the world just smear it over with a coating of salvation and all would appear lovely. The cut-throat and murderer whose garments are all dripping with the blood of slaughtered innocence takes a mouthful of this resolvent, is suddenly transformed into an angel of light and leaps from the gallows into the Kingdom.

If you get after a man for cheating you in a horse-track or if you have given him your name as surety in the load of money, or the payment of a debt, and you are left with the bag to hold, one sup from that slough will ease his conscience. Pay the debt and make his cup run over with happiness.

The resolvent that exudes from the slough is thick and ropy hung together like jelly. Although it is very obnoxious to the world and carnal minded because of his hidden virtues which are only known to the truly loyal and unadulterated few called the elect. It is an excellent remedy for the Lock Jaw; and for raising Cain has no equal. It strengthens the appetite, gives tone to the stomach and enlarges the capacity of the mouth for chicken. Sometimes it is only necessary for a small sprinkle to make you fascinating, and real good all over. I knew of man once who sat up all night trying to cheat his neighbor but as soon as he could be permitted to take a big drink at the fountain head his eyes were opened, and he saw his way clearly.

The people of this world that is the carnal minded know not the great value of the slough resolvent nor the first principles of salvation. Therefore cheat, lie and swindle as much as you please, only keep it well coated over, varnished with salvation.

Several photos (images) were also taken of the short story, Pisgah, taken from the same old handwritten book by William McFarland whose pen name was Wayside. These stories were all written before he died thus they are at least 123 years old. These photos all came directly from the originals and were made into black and white images suitable for printing into a book.

Mount Pisgah is a sublime place, and very high. The favored few are permitted to see the Land of Promise. ...olaries who try to climb the height sublime. But nearing the dizzy height, their faith fails them. But a large slough which surrounds the base has a wonderful effect on the optic ner purely, which enables them to see the Land of promise from The name of this slough is called salvation. It is shallow smell is very offensive, but nevertheless it is a great... The Curative powers of this slough water is truly wonderful how filthy you are, it will make your garments appear... Those who use that water need never use soap. There... who would steal and lie for Christ sake do at ... wallow in all kinds of filth and corruption, and ... ...externally would be...

...wardly, which enables them to see the Land of promise. The name of this slough is called salvation. It is the smell is very offensive, but nevertheless it is a great The Curative powers of this slough water is truly... how filthy you are, it will make your garments... Those who use that water need never use soap. ... who would steal and lie for Christ sake do at... wallow in all kinds of filth and corruption; Al vation applied externally would be made to noon day sun. The workings of trickery a been carried on for years has brought many a ...of Christ I could scar

...of pain and unhappiness, and when the close of...
...ternally would be sure to shine as bright as the...

The workings of trickery and jugglery which has
for years has brought many a soul to poverty and rags
...owers of Christ I doubt scarcely understand it. But after
...ugh which flows from the side of the hill and surges
...knocked under, I surrendered; I admitted that salvation
...ment of reform. It could make black, white, and white...
...as anything too filthy to be seen or known by the world
...with a coating of salvation and all would appear...
...throat and murderer whose garments are all...
...blood of slaughtered innocence takes a mouthfull
...suddenly transformed into an angel of light...

...smear it over with a coating of salvation and...
...rely. The cut throat and murderer whose garm...
...ipping with the blood of slaughtered innocence tak...
...this resolvent, is suddenly transformed into an a...
...aps from the gallows into the kingdom.
...If you get after a man for cheating you in a h...
...you have given him your name as surety...
...money, or the payment of a debt, and you ar...
...bag to hold, one sup from that slough will...
...pay the debt and make his cup run over with...
...the resolvent that exudes from the slough is th...
...together like jelly. And though it is very...

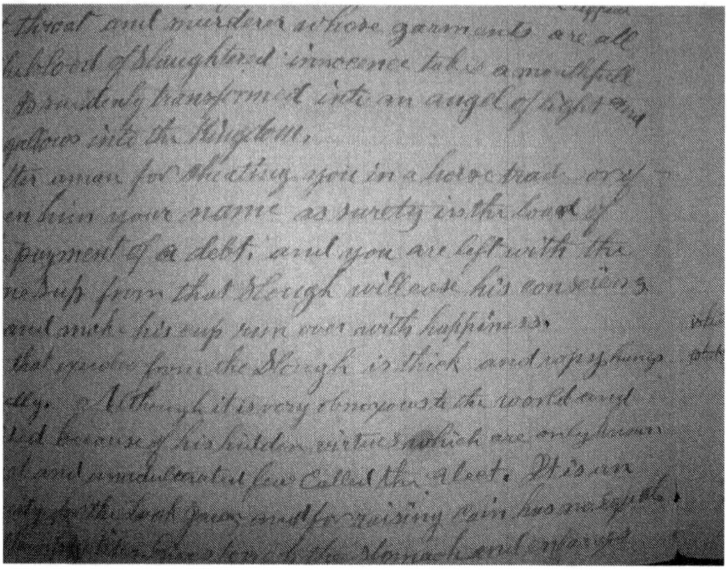

throat and murderer whose garments are all
blood of slaughtered innocence take a mouthful
suddenly transformed into an angel of light and
gallows into the Kingdom,
ter a man for cheating you in a horse trade or
n him your name as surety in the loan of
payment of a debt, and you are left with the
ne Sup from that Slough will ease his conscience
and make his cup run over with happiness.
that exudes from the Slough is thick and ropy hangs
lly. Although it is very obnoxious to the world and
ted because of his hidden virtues which are only known
l and unadulterated few Called the Elect. It is an
dy for the Lock Jaw and for raising Cain has no equal
[illegible]

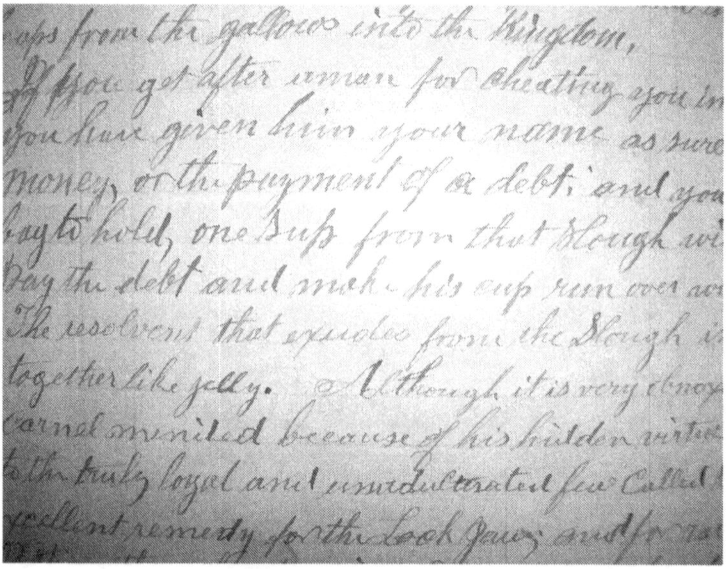

ps from the gallows into the Kingdom,
If you get after a man for cheating you in
you have given him your name as sure
money, or the payment of a debt, and you
hay to hold, one Sup from that Slough wi
pay the debt and make his cup run over wi
The resolvent that exudes from the Slough i
together like jelly. Although it is very obnox
carnal minded because of his hidden virtue
to the truly loyal and unadulterated few Called
excellent remedy for the Lock Jaw and for rai

CHAPTER THREE

WAYSIDE STORIES

MACHINE PRAYER

BY

WILLIAM MCFARLAND

'WAYSIDE'

July and August are gone and still there is no rain. This is the longest dry spell of weather known in these parts for years. Wells and cisterns are drying up. Is the perihelion or old mother Shipton responsible for this drought? Or are we so wicked that God won't hear the prayers of his dear children? Last winter we were snowed in and froze up; now we are scorched, burnt and dried up until there is but little left to be thankful for. Those persons who have faith as large as a grain of mustard, have a good chance to prove their faith by their works. Just start the Old Machine and let us have rain. We won't object if it is a small deluge; but if your faith is not large won't your prayers prove a mockery. Will God hear. Or does God too become a little deaf at times. This howling oneself hoarse to make a deaf God hear is nothing but rank superstition clothed with a pious mockery. But I must not be too hard on the Saints just now for they have a mighty big job on their hands already. President Garfield needs all their prayers, and it is very doubtful if their prayers will reach the throne of grace in time to save him. The people are honest and wish Garfield to live, but that prayer without works will cure a mortal wound is simply preposterous. This praying to God to save them from Arthur and conk ling borders on the ridiculous. Those pious frauds who voted for Garfield and Arthur last fall, with a whoop can't help but see that their prayers are nothing but mockery. We may be sincere and honest yet not one in ten thousand believes that God will answer his prayers. The sincerely pious think it is their duty when called on by someone in authority to lead in prayer. They try to fix up words suitable, wander on in a rambling jargon not even knowing what they ask for. This is the summon bon-run of all public praying. When one of those praying machines get down to business and prays mightily he knows that the people are listening and then he climbs higher, and higher, until all the gas with which is inflated is exhausted. Then he goes off into convulsions and rolls upon the ground. If you ask him what he prayed for, or, what he wanted he could not tell you. And if God would answer his prayer according to his request he would be most surprised and worse scared individual in the house. Good pious men sometimes pray not because they want to or that they are in need but because someone called on them in public and they did not like to refuse.

If the President dies of what avail is prayer? A perfect deluge of prayer has been poured out everywhere for his recovery. The Machine has been put to work and groaned mightily. Does Providence hear? Don't you think he is trying their faith a little too hard? If those theological drones should fail in this their last resort and extreme necessity. What respect can we have or any honest, intelligent man have for such a religion? Or what do such prayers amount to? It looks like Providence was a little slack or forgetful of his promises; or, that those theological individuals didn't understand the situation, or, did not know what they were praying for.

Prayer of the right kind of faith might save a sinner like Guiteau but will it save the President. Nine or ten weeks of incessant prayer would seem sufficient to reach the throne of grace and save most anybody. But wishing, hoping, and praying that God would condescend to visit earth and save Garfield is one of the isms of the Church that common people, especially the worldly minded can't quite understand.

It may be that Providence coincides with Arthur. If he does what are you going to do about it? Was it not the prayers of the faithful that put Arthur on the ticket? Didn't the clergy of Chicago meet in a body and pray to God to come down and run the convention? Did he not place his Vice gerent there to run the Machine if Garfield failed?

Now what does those this turning up of your noses against Arthur mean? Are you not all equally guilty? If Garfield dies can't Arthur and Guiteau run the Machine? Guiteau is one of the saints that believes in the Bible and prays much. O ye of little faith! Why are ye a stumbling block in the way of sinners?

The President is dead and the nation mourns. It is a Divinity that marks the course of all human events. But what has the prayers of the Church amounted to? Garfield is dead and that is all there is to it. All the prayers of the Church could not save him for they did not amount to a hill of beans. If their prayers had any virtue or saving grace in prayer Garfield would be living today. The people were honest and sincere. Garfield was prayed for as no man was ever prayed for. Did God hear? Did He answer? We sometimes pity the ignorance and gullibility of mankind. But this last attempt of the Machine to bulldoze the throne of grace to change the laws of nature and their signal failure is proof positive that their prayers never reached the courts above. Prayer without works is nothing but a humbug, a swindle and a cheat. Prayer as used or indulged in by some of our Orthodox quack divinities is nothing more nor less than rank superstition gathered from the musty records of heathen mythology.

The grave hath won its victim. But, Oh, what a blot does leave on the party and nation! What a foul stain on the pages of history! Murdered by the hands of those who helped to exalt him. Behold the dark form of the third term filling the background, standing as godfather to the incoming administration.

The ominous expression of the assassin, like Ban quos ghost rises to plague us with the words still ringing in our ears "Garfield is dead and Arthur is President." Momentous words and so full of meaning. Then, wind, change, and twist it as you will the Machine policy did it. There was an ambitious, wicked design in that killing for actions speak louder than words. Does any man say that Guiteau should not be hung? Then why this wrangling about the place of trial? This is the strongest proof in the world that long-headed cussedness is at the bottom.

Those who sow to the winds shall reap the whirlwinds, and those who have knaves and perjurers for bedfellows must howl with them. If they don't; there will be death in the pot.

President Hays was seated through lies and perjury and covered it over with the gift of office to servile fools who performed the dirty work. Many a good man was misled by those howlers. Most of the churches sold themselves to this demon of power and made themselves ridiculous by yelling "Hancock is a traitor and a rebel." The "Little man in black" rolled it under his tongue as a sweet morsel; a soothing syrup to quiet his nerves. Was there a truly loyal man that voted for Hancock? Was it not the unadulterated, the Simon pure who voted for Arthur, Guiteau and the third term? Was it not the Orthodox divinities who made those long winded prayers and appealed to the passions and prejudices of the ignorant? It is this kind of prayer that has caused most all the churches to wilt. There are many honest people in the party and in the churches who are almost ready to abjure the religion of their fathers. They see the *hideous deformity of the Machine and cover their heads for shame.*

God moves in a mysterious way; but one of our divines said that it was the devil that killed Garfield. This remark is in strange contrast with other notables (Divines) who say that God did it. Well, we will not quarrel with them about it, nor take sides. But this we will say; "It was a dastardly mean trick" no matter whether Guiteau, God or the Devil did it. This trying to palm it off on God or the Devil is done for the purpose of saving Guiteau's neck. It is a slur on Providence and an insult to the intelligence of the age. The death of Garfield is a natural product of the Machine. It was those long winded prayers of the Machine that done the dirty work.

Did God hear? Did he answer? No Sense
and gullibility of mankind. But this lust a
buildose the throne of grace to change th law
nal failure is proof positive that their their
Courts above. Prayer without works is nothing
and a cheat. Prayer as used or indulged
quack divinites is nothing more norless
gathered from the musty records of heathen

the grave hath won its victim But, Oh,
curse on the party and nation! What a fo
pages of history! Murdered by the hands
to exalt him. Behold the dark of the third [form]
back ground, Standing as god father t
administration.
The ominous expression of the assassin, like
to plague us with the words still ringing in
dead and Arthur is president; Momentous
of meaning. Turn, wind, Change, and
... thing policy did it. There was

...chine. Prayer.

Did he answer? We sometimes pity the ign[orance]
of mankind. But this last attempt of the machin[e]
...of grace to change the laws of nature and the...
...positive that their their prayers never reach...
...prayer without works is nothing but a humbug, a...
...Prayer as used or indulged in by some of our...
...es is nothing more nor less than rank sup[erstition]...
...musty records of heathen mythology.

...administration.
The ominous expression of the assassin, like...
to plague us with the words still ringing in o[ur]
...lead and Arthur is president, momentous...
of meaning. Turn, wind, change, and...
...the machine policy did it. There wa[s]
...wicked design in that killing for action...
...words. Does any man say that Guit[eau]
hung? Then why this wrangling abo[ut]
This is the strongest proof in the world th[at]
...cursedness is at the bottom.

...ntring as god father to the incoming

...tion of the assassin, like Banquo's ghost w...
...the words still ringing in our ears" Garfield...
...president, momentous words and so ful...
...n, wind, change, and twist it as you...
...olicy did it. There was an ambitious...
...n that killing for actions speak louder tha...
...ny man say that Guiteau should not b...
...hy this wrangling about the place of trial...
...est proof in the world that long-headed...
...the bottom.

...of meaning. wind, wind...
...the machine policy did...
...wicked design in that killing...
...words. Does any man s...
...hung? Then why this wra...
...This is the strongest proof in...
...cussedness is at the bottom.
...Those who sow to the wind s...
...have knaves and perjurers fo...

f the assassin, like Banquos ghost ris
rds still ringing in our ears" Garfield i
identy, momentous words and so fal
died, change, and twist it as ar el
did it. There was an ambitious,
killing for actions speak louder tha
an say that Guiteau should not h
is wrangling about the place of tria
oof in the world that long headed

hung? Then why this wrangling
This is the strongest proof in the worl
cussedness is at the bottom.
Those who sow to the winds shall reap the
have knaves and perjurers for bedfellow
If they dont; there will be death in the p
President Hays was seated through lies
it over with the gift of office to servile to
many a god may wipes misjo
work. Most of the churches sold them
power and made themselves ridyculous

...illing for actions speak louder than...
...an say that Guiteau should not be...
...wrangling about the place of trial...
...of in the world that long-headed...
...ons.
...I shall reap the whirlwinds, and those who...
...s for bedfellows, must howl with them...
...death in the pot...
...ted through lies and perjury, and covered...
...vise to servile tools, who performed their...

...ont; there will be death in the pot...
...t Hays was seated through lies and perjury...
...with the gift of office to servile tools who per...
...ny a ... ... missed by those...
...most of the churches sold themselves to the...
...and made themselves by yelling "ridgentous" Han...
...and a rebel," The "Little Man in B...
...r his tongue as a sweet morsel; a S...
...... Was there a truly loyal...
...coo.? Was it not the unadulterated...
...... for Arthur, Guiteau and th...

God moves in a mysterious; but one of ou
was the devil that killed Garfield. This rema
with other Notables (Divines) who say that God
not quarrell with them about it, nor take sides
"It was a dastardly mean trick, no matte
the Devil did it. I m this trying to pu
is done for the purpose of saving Guiteau a
dence and an insult to the intelligence of
the Death of Garfield is a natural produ
be same that seated Hays that killed
inded prayers of the Machine that done

Do this and you will be saved, but do
in the pot for vengeance is mine and I
X   X   X   X   X   X   X   X
The Machine hath Done its work and tho
return with a ghostly horror to plague
him,   X   X   X   X   X   X   X
Uneasily sits the president in the
a Martyred president is peering
Dimitz that mark the course of
Shall ye reap. Murder will
and

president in the Chair of state while the [Presi]
dent is peering over his shoulder. There
the course of all human events. As ye sow,
Murder will out. The truth though crush
e to plague the ~~murderers of the~~ medium
x x x x x x x x x x x x x x x
us. The dark days November days and the
come sighing over the the bleak plain proclai
ur pains and aches increase, and the cold
urback which sitting by the fire, tells the tale

indulgent lady; let not your heart
lieve in God so does Wayside,
lady; although we may differ in the
hr of a future state recollect that aw
possibly not in this world, but on the
river that flows down deep in the vale
your immortal spirit rises May w
welcome you to the Great By and By
ades and pleasures never die And
heavenly escort that shall wander
mountain of Light

CHAPTER FOUR

THE MACHINE

AND

THE CALF

BY

WILLIAM McFARLAND

'WAYSIDE'

In the days of Machine came Wayside preaching in the wilderness of Neponset City. And he opened his mouth and said unto the multitude that thronged round about trembling in their boots. O! Ye generations of Half-Breeds, Feather-heads, and Blainites. Why do you tremble? Who hath warned you to flee from the wrath to come? Now let everyone of you repent of your sins and cover your heads with sackcloth and ashes and make your crooked ways straight. Purge yourself of all self respect and swallow crow for the Machine is coming and off will go everyone of your heads unless you fall down and worship the Golden Calf which the Machine hath set up. You must bow down and worship at his feet and kiss his great toe. If you don't you all will be cast into outer darkness where there will be nothing but weeping, wailing and gnashing of teeth. You must get clear down on your knees, all of you and cry mightily, "Great is Providence. Great is the Machine and great is the Golden Calf which the Machine hath set up." Do this and you will be saved; but do it not and there will be death in the pot for vengeance is mine and I will repay saith the Machine.

The Machine hath done its work and those long winded prayers return with a ghostly horror to plague the running gear of the Machine.

Uneasily sits the President in the Chair of State while the ghost of a martyred President is peering over his shoulder. There is a Divinity that marks the course of all human events. As ye sow, so shall ye reap. Murder will out. The truth though crushed for a time and bleeding will rise to plague the Machine.

The winter is close upon us. The dark November days and the cold, chilling winds, as thy come sighing over the bleak plain proclaims the glom of Autumn. Our pains and aches increase, and the cold chill that crawls up our back while sitting by the fire, tells the tales winter is close upon us, yea it is even at the door.

Time, time, ever rolling ever changing in his sleep flight. How long, O how long will we have to wait? When will the harvest be? When will the bright star of hope that springs eternal in the human soul arise and shine? When shall eternal spring dawn upon us, when youth and beauty shall bloom forever more.

Why does the church complain of infidelity? Who are infidels? And what is it that makes mankind doubt the authenticity of the scriptures? Is it not the twisting and changings of the true meaning of God's Holy Word as given in the Bible? We are taught to believe that God never changes; that his Word is; and has been the same to all people. But somehow or other it did not suit the Machine. So it had to be revised under the instructions of the Machine. They found fault with its grammar and wasn't in accord with our modern civilization. This makes it rather hard on Providence. Makes him out an imperfect being like ourselves who have to learn by experience. This is what makes Infidels. Who wants to believe in a God that don't understand the languages, one that has to alter and change his word because the people are getting ahead of him? What respect can we have for a God that has to be run by a Machine? Or for such a book that needs a new version every time the Machine gets out of order. This is rock on which the Church split. This Machine worship, Machine gospel, Machine prayers with a Machine Providence to run things is too ridiculous for this intelligent age to receive.

It is said by some of those zealous perfectionists, those who pray as if they were going to take heaven by storm that Wayside is seriously tinctured with infidelity. Would say for the benefit of all concerned especially that good and noble lady of Sheffield Lake not to worry nor lose any sleep Wayside is no disciple of Bob Ingersoll, witch-craft nor the Devil, but talks of and takes things as he finds them. I am a firm believer in the earth as it is; but in regard to man's future, that is very difficult of comprehension.

I am of the earth earthly and as such will pass away; but what I shall be or what any man shall be is all a mystery not explained in the book of fate. The imaginations of mankind are very sketchy. When he comes to the incomprehensible, his mind like a stray comet flies off into space, seeking rest and finding none and like the story of the wandering Jew still keeps wandering.

Would say to the kind indulgent lady of Sheffield Lake, let not your heart be troubled. If you believe in God so does Wayside. Kind and gentle lady; although we may differ in this world on the philosophy of a future state recollect that we shall meet again possibly not in this world, but on the other side of the dark river that flows down deep in the valley of

*the death and as your immortal spirit
rises. May we be the first to greet and
welcome you to the Sweet By and By where
beauty never fades and pleasures never die
and may I be with that heavenly escort
that shall conduct to the Evergreen
Mountain of Light.*

...one you repent of you
with saccloth and ashes and make
Purge yourself of all self respect an
Machine is coming and of will
unless you fall down and wors
Which my lord Roscoe the king
bow down and worship at his fee
If you don't you all will be cast
where there will be nothing but
gnashing of teeth, You must get
... Mightily!! ...

...he opened his mouth and said unto the multitude that
...about trembling in their boots. O ye generations
..., featherheads, and Blairites, Why do you turn
...th warned you to flee from the wrath to come?
...ery one upon repent of your sins and cover your heads
... th and ashes and make your crooked ways straight
...f of all self respect and swallow Crow for the
...coming and of will, every one of your knees
...all down and worship the Golden image
...the Machine the king hath set up. You must
...nd worship at his feet and kiss his great toe
...ou all will be cast into outer darkness
...ill be nothing but weeping, wailing and
...th, You must get... in your house
...ry Mightily!! Great is Roscoe Great is the Machine

PART TWO

POEM BY WAYSIDE

In the last days of good James the trouble began,
When Stalwarts and Half-Breeds resolved each to damn;
The leaders locked wroth had blood in their eyes
'Twas then rule or ruin or the boat capsize
This trouble foretold the oncoming strife,
Of bloody, foul murder the President's life;
The people confounded through fear, and surprise
Not knowing from whence the next sacrifice

Come dramatic muse the darkness assail
And help me to raise the mystical veil
And gather new light from off the far shore
And learn how they run things for evermore
Twas in the last days of that trouble of Half-Breeds began
The dire sequence of the Stalwart clan
To kill and to stay all who dare come between
The loyal and brave who run the Machine

Thou light of my eyes - the banner unfurled
And let it wave grandly all over the world,
Gives hope to the soul gives light to the eyes
And learns people how to get rich, and be wise,
The idea is grand; its cause will inflate
Be true to the motto "vote early and late"
Will never betray whatever betide
Remember for us the Machine will provide

The doctrine is true, whatever we believe
So we cover our tracks the people deceive;
Talk strong in the faith of temperance too,
And ever keep flaunting the Ribbon of Blue
The world is fast sinking, clear out of sight
Soon they won't know the wrong from the light,
The only salvation is from the unseen
Which comes by the way of our Machine

The Glory World And Guiteau
by Wayside

Whenever nervous, feel sick, or feel dry,
Remember keep shady, and drink on the sly
Yes, drink all you want but shortly confess
That "Great is the mystery of godliness"
The Belial is grand and here let it be
A mystery profound, where no two agree
The only sure way to certain success
Is via the way of old Balaam's ass.

The Sons of Belial watch as we pass
And whispering say, "Come take a glass"
Dread craving desire it bothers us so
But drink with the friends we all have to do
It never would do in this vale of woe
To show safe way; 'tis plain to be seen,
Is stick to your friends who run the Machine.

Rejoice in the cause though trials do come,
Vote early and late but always keep mum;
For this is the way and always must be
To run the Machine where no two agree.
Remember the pious, be zealous, confess
That great is the mystery of godliness;
For this is the way to certain success and always must be
To run the Machine I have to confess where all men are free.

Discreet you must be and pious inclined
Be humble and low both reverend, kind;
Be kind to the church nor once let them think
You ever indulge in wine, or, strong drink,
The pious expect a harp and a crown
Reported for them in the Book of Renown
The old-fashioned Bible whose pages confess
That great is the mystery of godliness

The world is so gross they can't understand
The science of party in this favored land,
They blunder through life, not knowing from whence
Is the power derived we call "Providence"
But few in this world ever find out, or, know
The hollow workings of things here below;
But nothing so certain to give us success
As the great hue and cry of godliness

Poor ignorant souls cannot comprehend
The Sentence Divine that hangs over men
Their only salvation to them here is seen
Is stick to the ones who run the Machine
Must never give way to men of queer minds
To Half-Breeds, Feather-Heads, Bourbons, unkind
All enemies sure and ever hath been
To those loyal men who run the Machine.

This famous Machine has run long and well
But if you forsake it will send you to hell
Orthodox doctrine our friends we must screen
By voting for those who run the machine
Providence governs and rules on our side
The church and the Priests do in us confide
For Green-Bucks they all will barter the soul
And their birthright in Heaven will give for gold.

The Glory World And Guiteau
by Wayside

Money is king it rules everywhere
It rules church and state and also the fair
For prayers pay gold, divided between
The hypocrites, blubber and the Machine
The ignorant bow at the shrine of success
And pray very loud according to stress
They vote never doubting let naught intervene
To hinder the party or hurt the Machine

James Abram so good whom many applaud
And magnify greatly, most equal with God
It never would do to have him between
The flesh and the Del who run the Machine
You know in Degolier how grandly he rode
High and dry over all Mobilier he rode
We never could trust him nor have him between
The loyal and brave who run the Machine

Of things so uncertain here under the sun
It never would do to trust in that one!
A pious old fraud that dodges between
The law and the gospel and the Machine,
Poor Guiteau a crank, religious inclined
So wicked by zealous subtle and blind
Would aid and assist by making things even
And help us to send Guiteau and good Abram to Heaven

A bargain was made the contract was sealed
This poor foolish crank did willingly yield.
The good of the party demanded they said
A true, loyal Stalwart should stand at the head.
His price was so cheap a small porridge mess
Most nothing at all we had to confess,
But Providence kindly would call it sublime
And hide him in Glory World with the Divine.

James Abram and Guiteau so saint like and pure
Would honor the cause in Heaven that's sure
The Lord would take them and put them on trial
Exalted above all sons of Belial
The Stalwarts felt troubled resolved then to try
The grandest expose of knocking things high,
This poor Bible crank so servile and mean
Was used as a tool to run the Machine

They gave him a promise to serve as a blind
Would satisfy hunger and strengthen his mind
If he would act promptly, act on the sly
Have Abram to shuffle off quickly to die,
Never more will the Bourdons dare flaunt it again
Never more will we hear, or see the dread sign
That hateful odd number 329 (Three twenty nine)

Nevermore will it hurt our honor and pride
Nevermore will they dare to say that he lied
Nevermore will it be our duty to screen
Or hide him in Glory World with the Machine,
For promises given in Abram did ride
The Stalwarts resolved to be even
By the help of poor Guiteau they sent him to Heaven

Poor Guiteau was hung and some people say
The thing was all wrong it wasn't fair play
But la! that was nothing 'twas plain to be seen
'Twas done at the instance of the Machine
When all is secure and Arthur doth ride
Over all opposition exalted preside
Then all will be lovely, calm and serene
For that is the way with our Machine

Now we must be wise look harmless as doves
Be gentle and shrewd and deal in soft gloves
Must smile on the Sisters and fondly caress
The essence derived is exquisite bliss
Must flatter the church whenever we can
And make them believe we have the best plan
Come join our party be faithful and bold
And we'll build you a church and fill it with gold

The Glory World And Guiteau
by Wayside

The Blue Ribbon Brothers we'll hold by the hand
And get all the votes they have at command,
We'll canvass around young ones and old
And draw them all in with Green-Backs and gold,
Then all will be happy run smooth on our side
Good Arthur the Stalwart will with us divide
Be pious inclined, look calm and serene
And that is the way we'll run the Machine.

Soon we will call the party together
Proclaim it aloud "Forsake it? No never!"
But cling to the party whatever betide
Have faith and believe the Machine will provide
Now this is the way we all understand
To beat the Old Bourbons we hereby command
Just keep the way clear let naught intervene
To clog up the way, or, balk the Machine.

5

Whenever nervous, feel sick or f...
Remember keep shady, and dri...
Yes, drink all you want But...
That "great is the mystery of Go...
The Idea is grand and here le...
A mystery profound, where no...
The only sure way to certain...
Is via the way of old Bel...

6

The sons of Belial watch o'e...
And whispering say "Corre...
Drunk craving desire with...
...drink with the friends we...

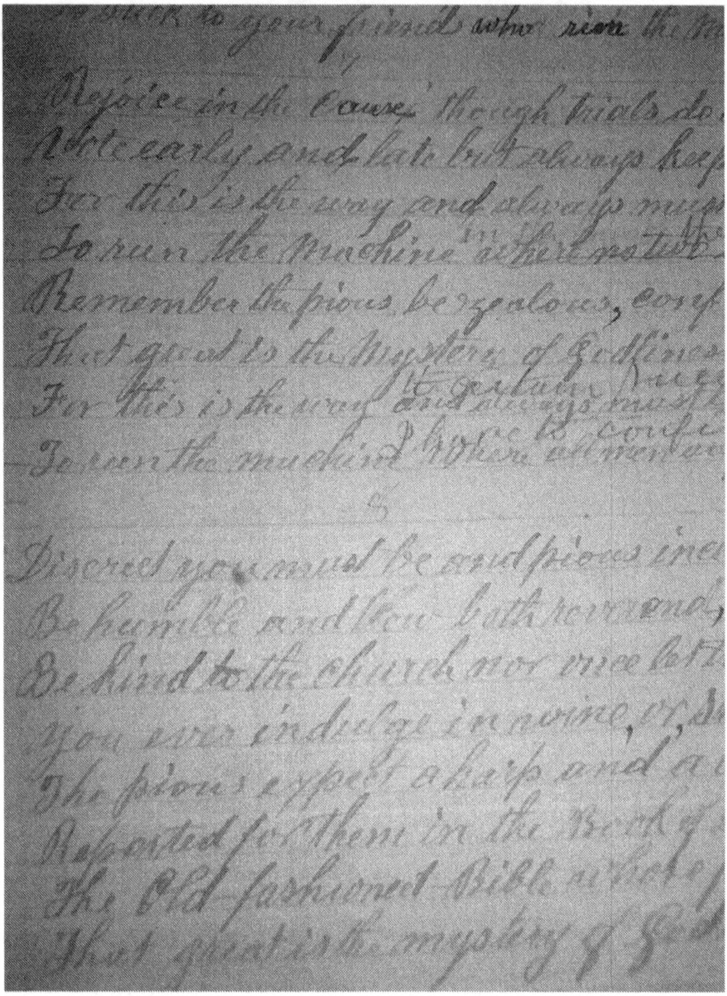
...stick to your friends who rise the...

4

Rejoice in the Cause though trials do...
Vote early and late but always keep...
For this is the way and always must...
To run the Machine in the where no two...
Remember the pious, be zealous, conf...
That great is the Mystery of Godlines...
For this is the way and always must...
To run the machine where all men are...

5

Discreet you must be and pious inc...
Be humble and bow both rev and...
Be kind to the church nor once let...
You ever indulge in wine, or S...
The pious expect a harp and a...
Reported for them in the Book of...
The Old-fashioned Bible which...
That great is the mystery of God...

The Machine

Whenever nervous, feel sick, or feel
Remember keep steady, and drink
Yes, drink all you want But s...
That great is the mystery of God...
The Patone is grand and here let...
A mystery profound, where no...
The only sure way to certain...
Is via the away of Old Bala...

The sons of Belial watch as we pass
And whispering say, "Come take a glass,
D... craving dear ... it bothers us...
But Drink with the friends we all have to...
It never would do in this vale of woe...
To show our hands, let all the world kn...
The only safe way, its plain to be se...
Is stick to your friends who ... the...

Rejoice in the Cause, though trials...

That great is the mystery of godliness

10

The world is so gross they can't understand
The science of party in this far cruel land
They blunder through life, not knowing from where
Is the power derived we call "Providence;"
But few in this world ever find find out, or know
The hollow workings of things here below;
But nothing so certain to give us success
As the great hue and cry of Godliness.

11

Poor ignorant souls cannot comprehend
The Sentence Divine that hangs over men

11

Poor ignorant souls cannot comprehend
The Sentence Divine that hangs over men
Their only salvation to them here is seen
To stick to the ones who run the machine
Must never give way to men of queer
The Flat Bicks, Southern bloods and Bour
All enemies sure and each hath been
Those Loyal men wherever the Un

12

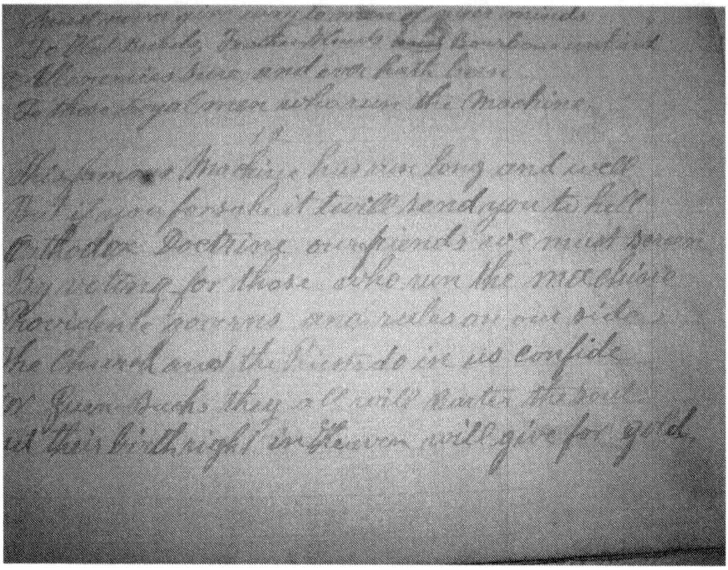

[illegible] minds
To [illegible] Bourbons [illegible]
All enemies here and ever hath been
To those loyal men who run the Machine.

11

This famous Machine has run long and well
But if you forsake it twill send you to hell
Orthodox Doctrine our friends we must [illegible]
By voting for those who run the machine
Providence governs and rules on our side
The Church and the Priests do in us confide
For Greenbacks they all will barter the soul
And their birthright in Heaven will give for gold.

Photo (image) taken by my own digital camera of the actual book cover that William McFarland (Wayside) wrote his stories and poems in. This book here shows the many pages and some of these stories and poems will are in other books by William McFarland (Wayside) which will be a series of books by Wayside entitled Wayside Stories. I am using his name on all of the books and not my own name.

The above photo is simply from the original book cover which shows the condition of the cover which held these writings for over 123 years along with the condition of the seam. They were written in a simple notebook and never published into a book to my knowledge!!

Close up of the actual signature by Wayside from the original writer of these stories! This way it is like an autograph at the end of this book!!